Pets

THIS EDITION
Editorial Management by Oriel Square
Produced for DK by WonderLab Group LLC
Jennifer Emmett, Erica Green, Kate Hale, *Founders*

Editors Grace Hill Smith, Libby Romero, Maya Myers, Michaela Weglinski;
Photography Editors Kelley Miller, Annette Kiesow, Nicole DiMella;
Managing Editor Rachel Houghton; **Designers** Project Design Company;
Researcher Michelle Harris; **Copy Editor** Lori Merritt; **Indexer** Connie Binder; **Proofreader** Larry Shea;
Reading Specialist Dr. Jennifer Albro; **Curriculum Specialist** Elaine Larson

Published in the United States by DK Publishing
1745 Broadway, 20th Floor, New York, NY 10019
Copyright © 2023 Dorling Kindersley Limited
DK, a Division of Penguin Random House LLC
24 25 26 10 9 8 7 6 5 4 3 2
003-334103-July/2023

A catalog record for this book
is available from the Library of Congress.
HC ISBN: 978-0-7440-7478-9
PB ISBN: 978-0-7440-7480-2

DK books are available at special discounts when purchased in bulk for sales promotions, premiums, fundraising, or educational use. For details, contact: DK Publishing Special Markets, 1745 Broadway, 20th Floor, New York, NY 10019
SpecialSales@dk.com

Printed and bound in China

The publisher would like to thank the following for their kind permission to reproduce their images:
a=above; c=center; b=below; l=left; r=right; t=top; b/g=background

123RF.com: Anatolii Tsekhmister / tsekhmister 12bc, 23bl; **Dreamstime.com:** Adogslifephoto 19br, Lars Christensen 7b, Alexandr Ermolaev 15bc, Linda Erwe 18br, Sonya Etchison 19bl, Eric Isselee / Isselee 6bc, Isselee 1b, 11bc, 15br, 23clb, Duncan Noakes 10-11, Irina Orlova 8-9, Svand 14-15, Shannon Tidwell 4-5; **Fotolia:** Eric Isselee1e 3cb;
Getty Images: DigitalVision / Oliver Rossi 21br, EyeEm / Ronnachai Palas 21bl, Moment / Catherine Falls Commercial 8br, Westend61 18-19; **Getty Images / iStock:** Nattapong Assalee 12-13, E+ / JLBarranco 14br, E+ / Michele Pevide 16-17, E+ / SolStock 22; S**hutterstock.com:** Chrisbrignell 9bl

Cover images: *Front:* **Dreamstime.com:** Tartilastock (Dogsx2), Valiva ca;
Shutterstock.com: D-sign Studio 10 cla, miniwide cl, Marta Sher crb, Malinovskaya Yulia (b/g)

All other images © Dorling Kindersley
For more information see: www.dkimages.com

For the curious
www.dk.com

Pets

Libby Romero

There are many kinds of pets.

Fish are pets.
Fish swim
in a tank.

fish

Hamsters are pets.
They can run
in circles.

hamster

A hermit crab
can be a pet.
It lives in a shell.

hermit crab

This rabbit is a pet.
It hops fast.

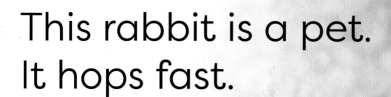

rabbit

These birds sing.
They are pets, too.

bird

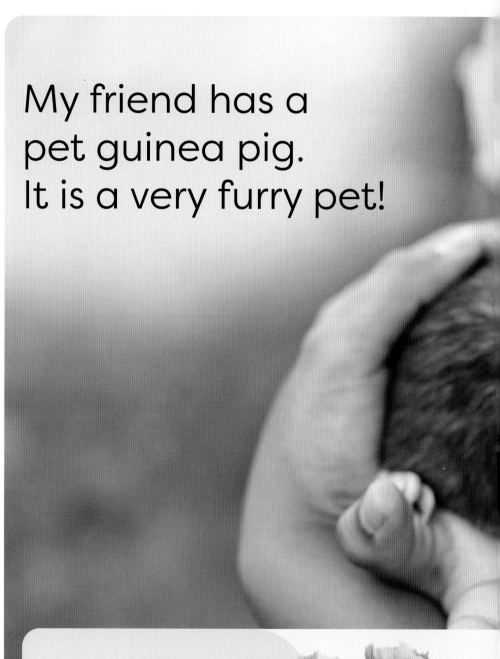

My friend has a
pet guinea pig.
It is a very furry pet!

guinea pig

I have a pet dog.
My dog does tricks.

dog

Woof! Woof!

My aunt has lots of kittens. She likes to play with them.

Meow!

kittens

Meow!

People love their pets.
Pets are part
of the family!

Glossary

bird
an animal with wings and a body covered with feathers

fish
a scaly animal with fins and gills that lives in the water

hamster
a small, furry animal with a round body and large pouches in its cheeks

hermit crab
a crab that lives in an empty shell to protect itself

rabbit
an animal with long ears and long hind legs

Quiz

Answer the questions to see what you have learned. Check your answers with an adult.

1. Which pet lives in a tank of water?

2. Which pet lives in a shell?

3. Which pet can hop?

4. Which pet can do tricks?

5. What is your favorite kind of pet? Why?

1. A fish 2. A hermit crab 3. A rabbit
4. A dog 5. Answers will vary